Peter and the Wolf

Peter and the Wolf

by Sergei Prokofiev
adapted by
Miguelanxo Prado

NANTIER · BEALL · MINOUSTCHINE
Publishing inc.
new york

8 7 6 5 4 3 2

ISBN 1-56163-200-7

Translation by Joe Johnson
Lettering by Martin Satryb
Printed in Spain

ETER AND THE WOLF is a folk tale. While folk tales are usually meant for children, they nonetheless possess a fascinating, evocative power for adults. As I began to work on this story, I found myself recalling fleeting, forgotten feelings with every brush stroke I used to create the world of Peter and his grandfather. I also discovered that the moral lesson contained in every folk tale could be brought up to date.

For me, it was marvelous to once again find that enigmatic light and that forest, those reflections of so many other attractive, almost dizzying, childhood dreams. Let's hope that my version of "Peter and the Wolf" will lodge a beautiful memory in some corner of little peoples' minds and will help big people re-discover that powerful sensation of mythical fears when, by the light of a small lamp, their grandmother or mother sat at the foot of the bed, us with the warm, protecting sheets pulled up to our noses, with our eyes wide open, looking beyond the stains of the ceiling, to the fascinating images of the story that they were telling.

Miguelanxo Prado

At the edge of an immense forest as vast as the sea, just like in a tale, stood a house.
A path ran from this house to a fence gate.
A road stretched away from that gate, leading into the forest in one direction and towards the hamlet in the other.

In that house, hemmed in by the fence and the forest, lived Peter and his grandfather.

Remember, Peter: never go far from home and especially don't ever go down the road.

And don't ever go into the forest for any reason, because you'll never come back out.

A ravenous wolf, as big as a hurricane, prowls in there.

Inside him, fear and an invincible attraction were brewing.

Just as vast as the forest.

The forest...

Peter awoke at the first glimmers of dawn.

He quietly went outside, followed the path and went out to the road.

A little bird perched on a tree branch greeted him with its flute-like trills.
♪

Good morning, Peter. You're up early.
Hello, little bird.

Together they followed the road into the forest. The forest smelled of the heavy, wet aroma of mosses and dead leaves; the sounds of a duck splashing in a pond hung in the air.
Where are you going, Peter? Didn't your grandfather forbid you to come into the forest?

A wolf, as big as a mountain, whose hunger is never sated, is hiding in the shadows.

Hmph! Coward's tales! Have you ever chanced to see him?

Those who have aren't around to tell about it, you foolhardy youngster.

The birds launched into a heated, noisy discussion concerning the possible advantages of going into or not going into the forest. Peter watched them without getting involved.

While the birds' argument went on interminably and Peter discovered the innumerable noises and sounds of the forest, they were unaware that something was approaching them.

First one step...

...Then another...

...yet another...

The little bird was the first to feel the sudden, strange presence and realized that danger was nearby.
♪...?

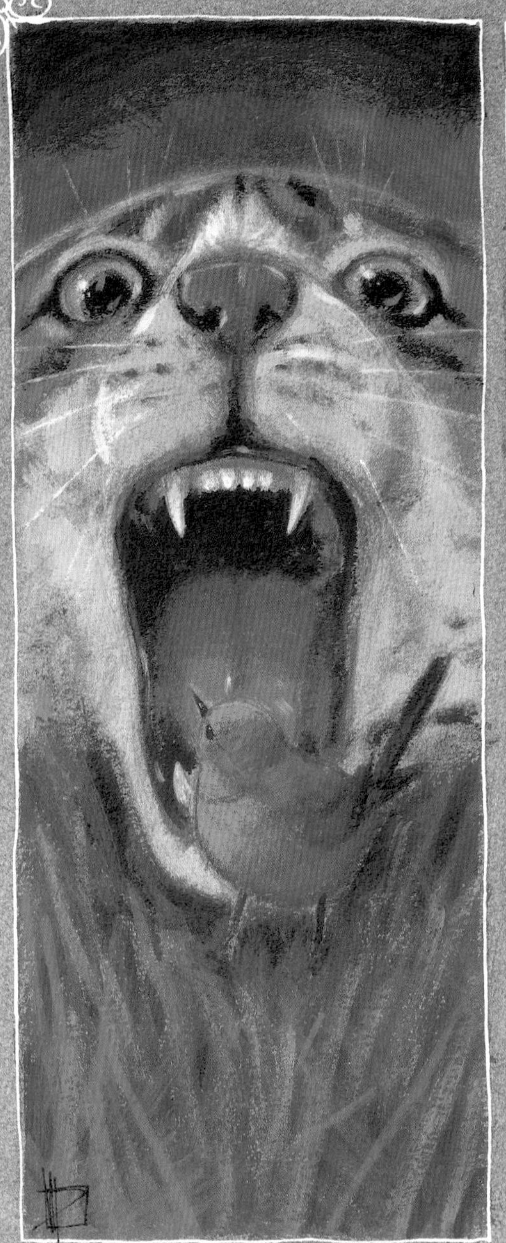

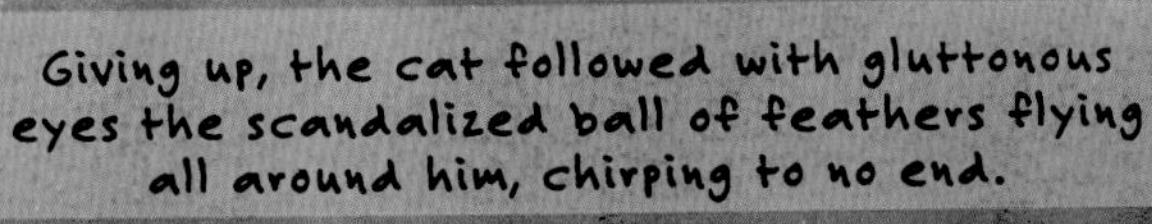
Giving up, the cat followed with gluttonous eyes the scandalized ball of feathers flying all around him, chirping to no end.

And the duck, put on her guard, kept an eye on the cat, watchful for the slightest motion.

The clamor rang
across the forest...

...in the chilly silence
of the morning.
Peter!

I see you didn't pay much attention to my advice!

I only...went in a little ways...

Do you think that the giant wolf which haunts this forest will care whether you went a few steps or a long ways inside? The fact is that you went in.

Far from the house and outside of the fence, nothing will stop him.

His hunger is as big as a winter night and
a little child like you will not satisfy him.

Peter was very impressed by
his grandfather's words.

But, before long, he told
himself that they were
quite exaggerated.

The forest was huge and surely the wolf was miles away hunting for something to appease his hunger.

Searching for defenseless prey.

Naive and unsuspecting.

Especially unsuspecting.

The little bird once again felt the same dread and swiftly flew off without even having glimpsed the wolf.
The cat felt it, too, and with a leap, climbed into the nearest tree before it realized what had driven him there.
The dread that Peter felt caused him to dash to the fence, stricken with a panic far stronger than his curiosity.
As for the Duck, it felt narry a shiver.

The wolf effortlessly swallowed her in one gulp.

In the forest's silence, all that could be heard were the racing heart beats of Peter, the cat and the bird, and the gorged rumblings of the wolf's belly.

Peter soon got a hold of himself and
decided to lay a trap for the
awesome, ferocious animal.

Two hunters were tracking the beast.

When they saw him, they were so excited that they didn't listen to Peter...

...Who was shouting at them that there was no reason to shoot.

The forest exploded.

Peter understood that his grandfather shared the same pain that he himself felt at that very moment.

It was a magnificent wolf and the forest was its kingdom. If only he'd followed his grandfather's advice, instead of...

But people are fickle.

And their vanity is as insatiable
as the hunger of wild animals.
Peter was no exception.

So that in place of the pain he'd felt about the wolf,
he now only felt the admiration that the entire hamlet expressed over his great feat. So it goes.